LOOKING AT
COUNTRIES

Looking at
JAPAN

Jillian Powell

Gareth Stevens
Publishing

Please visit our web site at: www.garethstevens.com
For a free color catalog describing our list of high-quality books,
call 1-800-542-2595 (USA) or 1-800-387-3178 (Canada).

Library of Congress Cataloging-in-Publication Data

Powell, Jillian.
    Looking at Japan / Jillian Powell.
        p. cm. — (Looking at countries)
    Includes index.
    ISBN-13: 978-0-8368-8171-4 (lib. bdg.)
    ISBN-13: 978-0-8368-8178-3 (softcover)
    1. Japan—Juvenile literature. I. Title.
    DS806.P68   2007
    952—dc22   2007003488

This North American edition first published in 2008 by
Gareth Stevens Publishing
A Weekly Reader® Company
1 Reader's Digest Road
Pleasantville, NY 10570-7000 USA

This U.S. edition copyright © 2008 by Gareth Stevens, Inc.
Original edition copyright © 2006 by Franklin Watts.
First published in Great Britain in 2006 by Franklin Watts,
338 Euston Road, London NW1 3BH, United Kingdom.

Series editor: Sarah Peutrill
Art director: Jonathan Hair
Design: Storeybooks Ltd.
Picture research: Diana Morris

Gareth Stevens managing editor: Valerie J. Weber
Gareth Stevens editors: Barbara Kiely Miller and Dorothy L. Gibbs
Gareth Stevens art direction: Tammy West
Gareth Stevens graphic designers: Charlie Dahl and Dave Kowalski

Photo credits: (t=top, b=bottom, l=left, r=right, c=center)
Stephan Boness/Panos: 12, 20. Paul Dymond/Lonely Planet Images: 13. Robert Essell NYC/Corbis: 7b. Joson/zefa/Corbis: 27b.
Catherine Karnow/Corbis: 11t. Karen Kasmanski/Corbis: 15t. Issei Kato/Corbis: 9. Charles & Josette Lenars/Corbis: 15b. Paul
Quale/Panos: 14. Chris Stowers/Panos: 17. Superbild/A1 Pix: 6, 11b, 25t, 25b, 26. Superbild/Incolor/A1 Pix: front cover, 1, 4, 7t,
8, 10. 16, 18, 19b, 21, 23, 24, 27t. Tom Wagner/Saba/Corbis: 22. Michael S. Yamashita/Corbis: 19t.

Printed in the United States of America

1 2 3 4 5 6 7 8 9 11 10 09 08 07

Contents

Words that appear in the glossary are printed in **boldface** type the first time they occur in the text.

Where Is Japan?

Japan is in Asia. The country is made up of four main islands and thousands of smaller islands in the Pacific Ocean.

Japan's capital city is Tokyo. It is on Honshu, which is the largest island. Tokyo has old palaces, **temples**, **shrines**, and gardens. It also has modern skyscrapers with offices, banks, and stores.

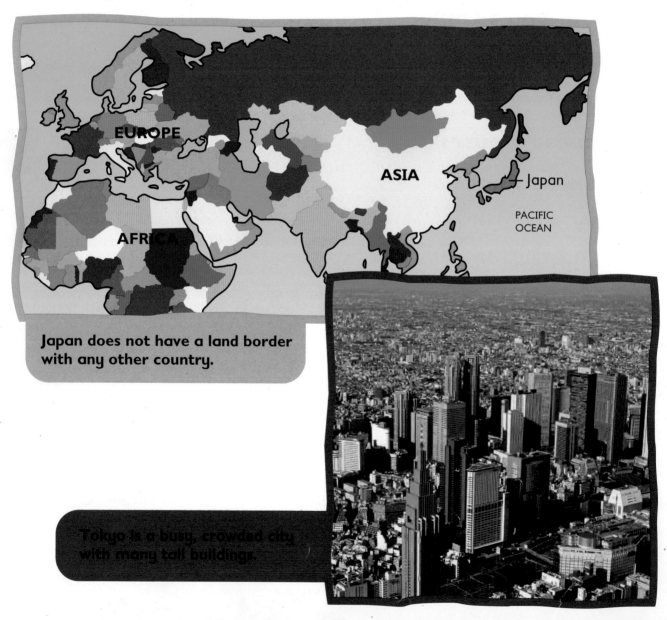

EUROPE

ASIA

Japan

PACIFIC OCEAN

AFRICA

Japan does not have a land border with any other country.

Tokyo is a busy, crowded city with many tall buildings.

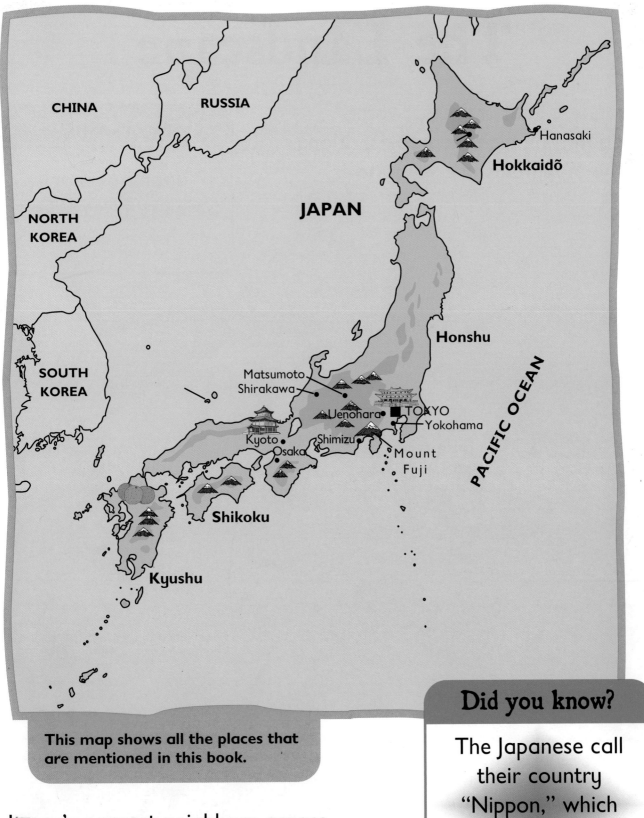

CHINA

RUSSIA

NORTH KOREA

SOUTH KOREA

JAPAN

Hokkaidõ

Hanasaki

Honshu

Matsumoto
Shirakawa
Uenohara
Kyoto
Osaka
Shimizu
TOKYO
Yokohama
Mount Fuji

PACIFIC OCEAN

Shikoku

Kyushu

This map shows all the places that are mentioned in this book.

Japan's nearest neighbors across the Sea of Japan are South Korea, North Korea, China, and Russia.

Did you know?

The Japanese call their country "Nippon," which means "Land of the rising Sun."

5

The Landscape

Japan is a land of lakes, rivers, streams, and high mountains. Many of the mountains are **volcanoes**.

At 12,388 feet (3,776 meters), Mount Fuji is Japan's highest mountain.

Thousands of people visit Biei in the summer to see its colorful fields.

Less than one-fourth of Japan's land can be used for farming. Most farms are in river valleys and on flat land along the coasts. Farmers grow fruits and vegetables and keep animals such as chickens. They grow rice in flooded fields called **paddies**, in **valleys**, and on **terraced** mountain slopes.

Rice grows on terraces near the city of Shimizu on Honshu.

Weather and Seasons

There are big differences in the weather between northern and southern Japan. The northern islands have long, cold winters and short, warm summers. They can have lots of snow and ice in winter, especially in the mountains.

In the south, the weather is warm all year round. Winters are mild, and summers are hot. Rain falls mostly between June and September.

Did you know?

The Japanese hold parties to view cherry tree blossoms in the spring.

Oranges grow in the warm climate of southern Japan.

A typhoon hit the island of Nakanoshima and flipped this car.

From September to November, Japan can have tropical storms called **typhoons**. They bring heavy rains. **Tidal waves** flood in from the Pacific Ocean and can cause lots of damage.

Japanese People

The Japanese are proud of their **culture** and traditions. They believe in working hard. Respect for others, especially older people and family **ancestors**, is also important to most Japanese. Most homes have a special place or room where people pray to their family ancestors.

This building is a Buddhist temple. There are more than one thousand Buddhist temples and Shinto shrines in Kyoto.

Japan's main religions are **Buddhism** and **Shinto**. Many Japanese pray at temples or shrines, especially at important times such as a wedding or the birth of a child.

A monk rakes stones in a Zen garden. Zen is a form of Buddhism.

This woman carries out the tea ceremony in Kyoto. She is wearing a traditional Japanese **kimono**.

The **tea ceremony**, called *chanoyu,* is a popular Japanese tradition. It is a special way to make tea and was first practiced by Buddhist monks. It is now taught at tea clubs and schools. People use this ceremony to entertain their family and friends and tourists visiting Japan.

School and Family

Japanese children must start school when they are six years old. Many begin school at three or four years old, however. The school day begins at 8:30 a.m. and ends at 4:30 p.m. All children wear school uniforms and study the same subjects. They learn to read and write Japanese and one other language, often English. At the end of each day, children clean up their classrooms before going home.

Children attend elementary school for six years. Then they go to junior high school, or secondary school, for three years. Many continue their education in high school and beyond.

This girl is wearing a secondary school uniform.

Using **chopsticks,** members of this family serve themselves from a big pot of food on the table.

Today, many Japanese parents have only one or two children. Aunts, uncles, and grandparents may live with the family, too. Everyone plays their part in family life. Most families share a meal together in the evening.

Did you know?

About four out of ten Japanese families have pets at home. The most popular pets are dogs, followed by cats and fish.

Country Life

In the Japanese countryside, many people live on small family farms. They may grow rice and another crop such as apples.

Everyone helps with farming, including the grandparents and children. After school and during vacations, children may help with jobs such as feeding chickens or pigs.

This man is planting rice seedlings using a small machine.

Did you know?

Bears live in the wild in parts of Japan.

These women are harvesting tea by hand.

It is traditional for Japanese mothers to carry their babies on their backs. Some women may do this when they are working in the fields.

On some farms, planting and harvesting is done by hand. Other farmers own small machines or share larger machines with their neighbors. Many country people only farm part-time. They do other jobs to earn more money. Along the coasts, for example, people go fishing or gather seaweed to eat.

City Life

Four out of five people in Japan live in towns or cities. Most of Japan's big cities are on or near the Pacific coast. Tokyo, Yokohama, and Osaka are the largest cities. The Imperial Palace, the home of the Japanese **emperor**, is in Tokyo.

These skyscrapers are in Yokohama. This busy city is on the island of Honshu.

People in Tokyo rush to work. Some are wearing face masks to protect themselves from pollution.

Many people live busy lives in Japan's cities. They use the latest high-tech inventions, go to Western-style stores, and eat fast food.

Japan's cities have good public transportation systems, including buses and underground trains. Traffic jams, air **pollution**, and overcrowding are problems in the cities, however.

Did you know?

People called "pushers" squeeze passengers onto underground trains during busy times of the day.

Japanese Houses

Traditional old houses in Japan are built from wood and have paper windows. Inside, thick rice-straw mats, called tatami, cover the floors. Paper or **bamboo** screens usually divide the house into rooms.

Did you know?

Japanese people leave their shoes next to their front doors to keep the tatami clean.

Roofs made from plants cover these traditional Japanese houses in the village of Shirakawa.

In the cities, most people live in small apartments in tall buildings. In the **suburbs**, some people live in apartments in shorter buildings. Other people live in separate houses with gardens.

Many people live in the suburbs and travel into Tokyo to work. This suburb is near Uenohara.

These apartment buildings in Osaka have balconies. People often hang their laundry outside to dry.

Japanese Food

Fish, vegetables, rice, and noodles are all important foods in the Japanese diet. People also use soybeans a lot in their food. Meat such as chicken and pork is cooked in stews. People also cut meat into thin strips and cook it with vegetables.

Sushi is a popular type of fast food in cities. Western-style fast foods such as hamburgers are also common.

A sushi bar is popular with city workers.

This food stall in a Tokyo market sells fresh fish.

Many people in Japan buy fresh foods from small stores or outdoor markets. In towns and cities, people shop at supermarkets, too.

At home, many families eat traditional meals, sharing several small dishes of different foods. They sit at low tables and use chopsticks to eat.

21

At Work

The main industries in Japan produce iron, steel, ships, cars, motorcycles, and electronic goods. These electronic goods include cell phones, computers, cameras, and televisions. Many brands of Japanese cars and electronic goods are sold around the world.

Did you know?

In the past, people in other countries sometimes said that the Japanese worked too much. In recent years, however, most people in Japan worked fewer hours.

This woman works at a cell-phone factory near Tokyo.

This man is unloading fish at Hanasaki's harbor on the island of Hokkaidõ.

Japanese people also work in banks, stores, schools, hospitals, and in transportation and farming. Fishing is a huge industry in Japan. Many fish farms also line its coasts. These farms produce fish, shellfish, and seaweed to eat.

Having Fun

Baseball, football, basketball, and golf are all popular sports to play and to watch in Japan. Japanese **martial arts** are taught in schools and clubs. These sports include tae kwon do, judo, and **kendo**. **Sumo** wrestling is also a popular sport for the Japanese to watch.

These children are practicing kendo in Matsumoto.

During the August Lantern Festival, people carry giant paper and bamboo lanterns. The lanterns are shaped like Japanese heroes.

Some people in Japan enjoy going to the theater. Kabuki is a traditional theater that tells stories of Japan's past. Actors wear colorful make-up and costumes. Young people enjoy watching television, playing computer games, and **karaoke**.

Colorful festivals throughout the year celebrate special times such as the rice harvest. There are ceremonies, parades with floats, lanterns, fireworks, feasts, and dancing.

These children are taking part in a rice-planting festival in Tokyo.

Japan: The Facts

- In Japan the emperor is the **head of state** and the prime minister leads the government. The Japanese people elect members of the Diet. This group makes laws for the country.

- Japan is divided into forty-seven different regions. Each region has its own governor.

- Japan has a population of more than 127 million people.

- Eleven cities in Japan have populations of more than one million people. The largest city is the capital, Tokyo. More than twelve million people live in the city and its suburbs.

The Japanese flag shows a red circle on a white background. This symbol is called the rising sun.

Japan's high-speed trains run between Tokyo and other major cities.

Did you know?

In Japan, May 5th is a holiday called "Children's Day." People celebrate the health, growth, and happiness of children.

The Japanese currency is the yen.

Glossary

ancestors – family members who lived in the past

bamboo – a tall plant with hollow, woody stems

Buddhism – a religion based on the teachings of Buddha, who lived from about 563 to 483 B.C.

chopsticks – a pair of thin sticks used for eating

culture – the way of living, beliefs, and arts of a nation or a specific group of people

earthquakes – shaking and cracking of the ground caused by movements in the rocks below the earth's surface

emperor – the male ruler of a country or empire

head of state – the main representative of a country

karaoke – singing songs along with a music recording

kendo – a Japanese sport of fencing using bamboo swords

kimono – a long, loose robe that has wide sleeves and is tied with a wide sash.

martial arts – sports of fighting and self-defense

paddies – fields that are flooded with water for growing rice

pollution – dirt in the air, on land, or in bodies of water that is caused by waste and chemicals from people and businesses

Shinto – a Japanese religion based on the worship of nature spirits and ancestors

shrines – places or buildings where people pray to a saint or a god in Shinto and other religions

suburbs – areas outside of large cities made up mostly of homes

sumo – a Japanese form of wrestling between two men

sushi – cold rice made into different shapes and served with sauce and small pieces of fish and vegetables

tea ceremony – the traditional art of making and serving tea

temples – buildings for prayer in Buddhism and other religions

terraced – cut into steplike levels or fields

tidal waves – huge, ocean waves that crash onto areas along the coast, causing floods and other kinds of damage

typhoons – tropical storms with very high winds

valleys – narrow areas of low land between hills or mountains

volcanoes – mountains made of dust, ashes, and melted rock. Hot gases deep underground forced these materials through the Earth's crust.

Find Out More

Kids Web Japan
web-japan.org/kidsweb

Say It in Japanese
web-japan.org/kidsweb/say.html

Kid's Life in Chichibu
www.ksky.ne.jp/~akihiroh

Publisher's note to educators and parents: Our editors have carefully reviewed these Web sites to ensure that they are suitable for children. Many Web sites change frequently, however, and we cannot guarantee that a site's future contents will continue to meet our high standards of quality and educational value. Be advised that children should be closely supervised whenever they access the Internet.

My Map of Japan

Photocopy or trace the map on page 31. Then write in the names of the countries, bodies of water, islands, cities, and mountains listed below. (Look at the map on page 5 if you need help.)

After you have written in the names of all the places, find some crayons and color the map!

Countries
China
Japan
North Korea
Russia
South Korea

Bodies of Water
Pacific Ocean
Sea of Japan

Islands
Hokkaidō
Honshu
Kyushu
Nakanoshima
Shikoku

Cities
Biei
Hanasaki
Kyoto
Matsumoto
Osaka
Shimizu
Shirakawa
Tokyo
Uenohara
Yokohama

Mountains
Mount Fuji

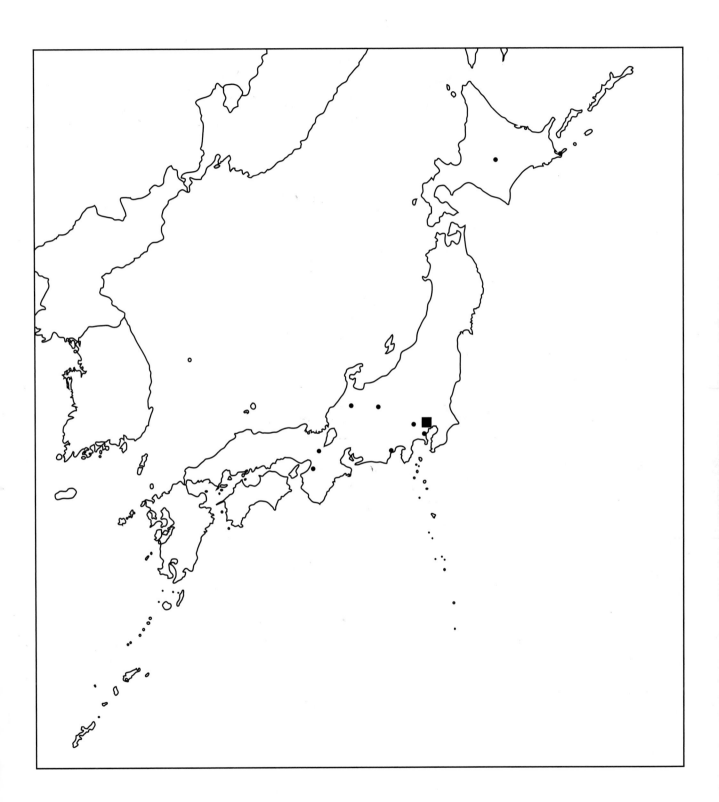

Index